Dedicated to Sirius. May the world be a better place by the time you're grown.

Printed in the United States of America

First Printing, 2013

ISBN-13 978-0615867045
ISBN-10 0615867049

Michigan Cannabis Business Association
4370 Chicago Drive SW #119
Grandville, MI 49418

www.StinkySteve.com

"My dad works long days
And when he comes home,
He goes into the bathroom
And sits there alone.

He comes out hungry,
Smelly, and ready to play.
And if he doesn't work,
He does it many times a day

If he took a drug test,
I don't think he'd pass.
Is my dad a junkie
Like we learned in class?"

"In school they tell us
That all drugs are bad
My mom's buying weed
And it makes me so sad.

Teacher said we should tell her
The nurse, or the cops
So that people can help her
And get her to stop.

What should I do?
Should I tell someone else?
She might go to jail!
I can't decide for myself."

"My granny takes care of me,
She loves me so much.
So why does she have drugs
Which she says I can't touch?

I thought drugs were for people
Who are mean and crazy.
But my granny's no pothead
And she sure isn't lazy!

I don't understand it,
I wish that I did.
Can someone explain it?
I'm only a kid!"

"With a pop and a flash
And a flick of my tail
My magic and answers
Help kids without fail!

There's no need to sob
And there's no need to wail!
Your parents aren't bad guys
Who should be in jail.

I'm Stinky Steve,
And I'm here to explain
That cannabis is a medicine
For grown-ups with pain."

“But Stinky Steve, I don't get it!
We learned in our schools
That drugs are for losers
And they're against the rules!

They said, 'Call it cannabis,
Ganja, weed, grass, or pot
It's criminal to grow it
Or use it, like it or not.

'It blackens your lungs
And kills cells in your brain
And if you smoke too much
You might go insane!'”

DRUGS ARE BAD, MMKAY
ganja, weed, grass, pot
① illegal
② blackens lungs
③ kills brain cells
④ insanity?
D.A.R.E.

"Some drugs are dangerous
And taking them becomes habit.
Hard drugs make you want more
And turn you into an addict.

Like they told you in class,
Illegal drugs make you sick.
But cannabis isn't a drug;
It's a green flower you pick.

What you learn in school
Is behind the times
In many cities and states
Cannabis is no longer a crime!"

"Cannabis is natural
And once you're grown up it's okay.
But don't take it from me!
Here's what others will say:

Doctors, lawyers, judges,
And smart scientists too
Have reviewed cannabis,
And they think it's fine to do,

If a grown-up has cancer, Crohn's,
Or an awful wasting disease,
Chronic pain, insomnia,
Or other serious issues like these

In some states with good laws,
Their doctor can legally say
'Medical marijuana is better for you
Than taking pills every day.'"

"Manuel, your daddy
Works hard on the line
Building pieces of cars,
But it's rough on his spine.

After working so hard
His poor back is burning,
And he needs medical help
To keep working and earning.

Instead of a pill for his muscles
And another for pain,
Your dad just has a puff
To feel better again."

"Christa, your mother
Just can't get to sleep
And when she's feeling blue
She forgets to eat.

Instead of some pills
That would make her a zombie
Your doctor understood;
Cannabis could help your mommy.

It helps her calm down
And it quiets her head.
She's too busy to grow it,
So she buys it instead."

1:23 AM

“Angel, your granny
Has glasses, you know
But I don't think she told you
The reason why, though.

Granny has glaucoma,
Painful pressure in her eyes.
The cannabis is from her doctor,
She never told you lies.

Because you're young,
It's not safe for you.
For grown-ups it’s safe
And better than pills too.”

"Smoking when you're young
It isn't cool and it isn't a joke.
Your brain is still growing
And things can get broke.

Wait until you're twenty or so
And all done with school.
And then if you need it,
Cannabis is a medical tool!

If you're worried about morals,
Just so you know,
Some religions ban booze,
But none ban things you can grow!"

"With a wiggle of my ear
And a flash of green light
I'll send you all home
Feeling better tonight!

Remember to follow
Stinky Steve's safety plan:
Don't touch the meds,
And don't tell The Man."

Please talk to your loved one
About what they do.
They'll say cannabis helps them
And that they'll always love you!

STINKY STEVE'S MEDICAL CANNABIS SAFETY TIPS FOR KIDS

- Follow Stinky Steve's safety plan: Don't touch the meds, and don't tell the Man.
- "The meds" are cannabis in any form and any devices someone uses to take cannabis. If cannabis or a cannabis tool or device is left where you can reach it, please tell a loved one right away!
- Common forms of cannabis include dried flower, capsules, kief, hash, concentrates, and medicated food items. Talk to your loved one about what kinds of cannabis they use.
- Tools for cannabis use include lighters, torches, grinders, pipes, glass smoking pipes, vaporizers, e-cigarettes (also called personal vaporizers), rolling papers, hemp wick, or special devices for concentrates. Never touch them; they could be hot!
- If your loved one uses medicated foods, be sure to talk about where they keep their medicated food and how it is labeled. Labels with the words medical, marijuana, dosage, THC, cannabis, medible, or similar language mean you should not touch it. When in doubt, always ask before eating something unfamiliar.
- "The Man" is anyone who might not understand medical cannabis. This can include your neighbors, other family members, teachers, doctors, and law enforcement.
- Because cannabis is medicine, your loved one deserves privacy. You should only talk about cannabis with your loved one who uses it or people they have told you specifically are okay.
- Some people still think cannabis is wrong, others may think it means they will find valuables if they break in to a house. No one you don't know or trust should ever be told about cannabis.
- To protect your loved one, do not talk to law enforcement about cannabis unless your loved one or legal guardian is with you. Unless you called them for help, you shouldn't talk to law enforcement alone. If law enforcement approaches you, ask for your parent/guardian immediately and don't answer questions. It's your right, use it or lose it!

STINKY STEVE'S MEDICAL MARIJUANA SAFETY TIPS FOR GROWN-UPS

- Any child old enough to understand cause and effect should receive basic cannabis safety instructions: teach them to never touch cannabis or cannabis tools, and to not talk about cannabis in public or with people you haven't specifically approved.

- While cannabis is safer than many household items, it still poses a risk to children. Cannabis and cannabis tools should be kept well out of the reach of children (especially infants), and should be in a locked case when not in use. A simple travel lock on a backpack stored on an upper closer shelf can suffice.

- Show children the forms of cannabis you use, as well as your tools. Explain that the children should never touch these items or try to use them. Children should be taught to report to adults immediately if cannabis or cannabis tools are found within reach.

- Take extra care with lighters, torches, and concentrate pipes, as they pose addition risk of burns.

- If you use cannabis capsules, pills, medibles, or juice, store the items out of the reach of the children, preferably in a locked cabinet or special drawer in the fridge.

- All medibles should be clearly labeled and kept in a designated locked location that the child knows about but does not have access to for safety reasons.

- If you grow your own cannabis, ensure your family has a practiced fire evacuation and safety plan. Teach your child the importance of never telling anyone about your garden to prevent the risk of crime or theft. Lock your grow room and keep all trim, trimming devices, and growing materials and chemicals out of the reach of children.

- Make sure your child understands how to interact with law enforcement. Teach them about their rights and the ongoing misperception of cannabis users.

- If you make concentrates, children should never be present. Concentrates should not be made in a residence, especially one where children live.

This book was made possible by the amazing Joel Tauchen. He is a super-star! We would also like to thank Kristine and Dave Fletcher, Kevin Smith, Jeni Juarez, Laurie Jared, Maria Page, Brad Clay, Deb Parrish, Alison Murphy, and Emily Jarrell.

Made in the USA
Charleston, SC
18 August 2013